# DAY IN SEARCH OF HER NIGHT/KNIGHT

Written and Illustrated by
**CLARE ROSENFIELD**

DAY IN SEARCH OF HER NIGHT/KNIGHT

Published by Gatekeeper Press
2167 Stringtown Rd, Suite 109
Columbus, OH 43123-2989
www.GatekeeperPress.com

Copyright © 2023 by Clare Rosenfield

All rights reserved. Neither this book, nor any parts within it may be sold or reproduced in any form or by any electronic or mechanical means, including information storage and retrieval systems, without permission in writing from the author. The only exception is by a reviewer, who may quote short excerpts in a review.

ISBN (paperback): 9781662935046

# Chapters

| | | |
|---|---|---:|
| Chapter One | **Prelude** | 1 |
| Chapter Two | **Imponderables** | 5 |
| Chapter Three | **The Search** | 9 |
| Chapter Four | **The Way In: Feeding The Serpents** | 24 |
| Chapter Five | **Incubating The Dream** | 36 |
| Chapter Six | **Homecoming** | 48 |
| Chapter Seven | **Meeting Her Muse** | 51 |
| About The Author | | 62 |

# CHAPTER ONE

# PRELUDE

She moves grace fully in the dark
Blending in with the velvety texture of Night,
Her sacred sensuality a mirror of the space
Night shapes of her in himself.

In fact Night is her lover,
Opens arms for her to burrow into.
At times Moon tries to peek in
Revealing this clandestine private partnership.
The two are not disturbed
Focused as they are
Intent on allowing the Revelation,
The unfoldment,
The gradual evolution of a gestation
Allowing each other

2

Herself and Night
To play
    experiment
        taste
            dive deep
Inspire and seed a new beginning,
The birth of a creation
As yet unknown to the world.

These two are chosen ones
Secret-keepers and
Receivers of divine gifts
Entrusted with them as a blessing to all of life.

Night dresses her in shiny winged garments
That she may love her gracious shimmering free-flowing form
And affords her both protection
And impetus to go forth courageously
To her/his destiny.

Once dressed, she watches transfixed
As Night transforms as well
Into her Knight,

The shadow to her light,

The body to her spirit,

The enactment of her passion.

Together they go forth to make all dreams

Of beneficence come true.

4

But first he asks, "May I know your name?"
"Jai," she responds. "It means Heart."
"Ah," he sighs, "It is good and right."

## CHAPTER TWO
# IMPONDERABLES

Dawn arises and lo her Night/Knight is nowhere
To be found.
She needs him, else feels incomplete,
Even bereft, destitute,
Naked, unsupported.

Sun tries to comfort her,
Seduce her, let her know that it is warmth and light
She loves, not just Night.

Jai fends him off,
"No," she cries, "my loyalty is with my knight,
My hero who melds his shape
Into mine and makes us
One."

Sun, in his rational way, explains,
"My dear, it is my reflection in moonshine
Then, that you respond to.
You delude yourself."

"No, no," she exclaims,
"Your light blinds me. It is in the darkness that all of me
And my seedlings grow, evolve, burgeon,
Stir the creative soil of my being.
Birth takes place underground,
In the moist loam of my innermost knowing."

"All right, I surrender," offers Sun. "But see,
You don't need Night/Knight for that.
You are already full of potential,
Capable of completeness."

"Oh, dear Sun, I know you are doing your best
To help me,
But Night is my lover,
The one who impregnates my seeds,
Who caresses me and blesses me.
He and I are pals,

"Inseparable like twins.
When he is not here,
I must journey forth to find him."

"Silly girl, he is always here,
He is always here,
Inside your innermost.
You yourself told me this,
That your seeds are burgeoning
In the depths, the dark depths of your being."

"O Sun, there is some mystery here
I don't fully understand.
You and I each have a portion
Of the truth,
A tiny glimpse perhaps.
I must go on my way to find the rest of this
And unravel this quest.
Am I whole unto myself?
Or am I only whole when in the arms
Of my Night/Knight?"

## CHAPTER THREE

# THE SEARCH

Jai follows her guide, in the form of her magical horse, her special steed,
Toward a beautiful valley. She is excited to discover what is there.
She feels that whatever is there will offer her an answer, a healing.
As they pass a group of blossoming orange trees wafting an enticing scent,
She hears a long beautiful "Ommmm." She stops and listens intently.
It is a sign, she feels, that they are on the right path.

Jai and her steed begin to pick up speed and gallop off to the distant mountains
In search of the answer.
Was her burgeoning, her completeness dependent on her lover?

Or was it the discovery of her own inner truth?
She heard a voice, a song, a deep sound luring her forward,
Awakening a longing,
Proferring an invitation.
Again, she was mystified.
From whence this sound, this calling?
From a distant Beloved?
From her own soul and spirit?

"Come, my Beloved,
Enter,
For in this abode,
There is nought but my longing for Thee."

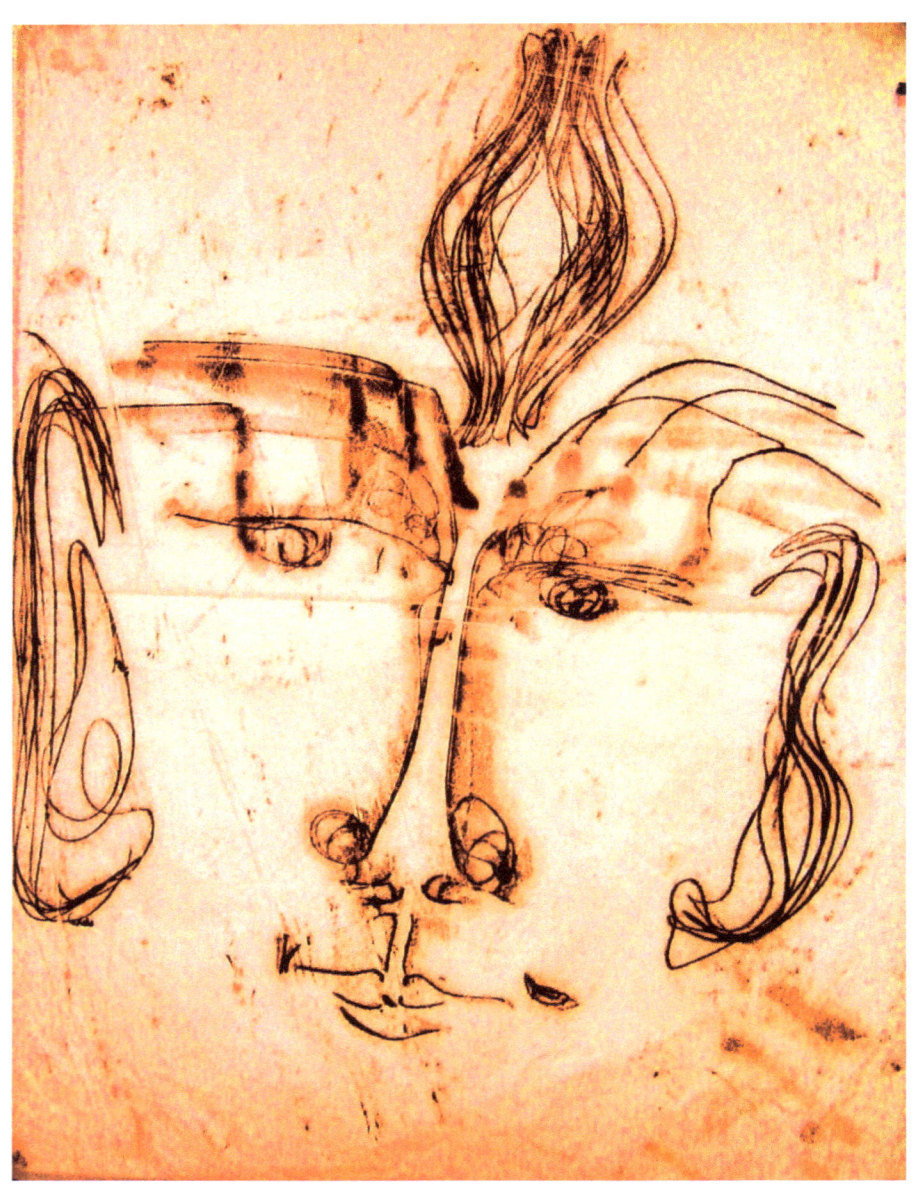

Crickets sing this song in her ears.
Birds above are chirping it too
And it seems to her that wings whirring by her
Swish these love-soaked pulsations
Into her racing increasingly ecstatic and curious heart.

"Someone wants me!" she exclaims.
"Someone is calling me his/her Beloved and longs for me.
Who can this be?"

"It is I who calls thee!" she hears inside her heart.

"Where dost thou live?" She queries.

"I live by the dunes, by the seas,
The better to feel the breezes caress my cheeks and tousle my curly locks.
I float my body upon the waves and am rocked
By the breaths of Earthmother, in the bosom of her circulating rhythms."

"Art thou a mermaid?" Jai asks.

"Oh, perhaps thou couldst call me that!
For truly I am in love with ocean, its deeps, its salty brine,

14

"Its rejuvenating powers, its welcoming of the graceful swans and ducks,
But the mountains too call to me and at times
I become one with the deep woods
Where I can turn into a tree nymph
And nestle in close to the ground, bark, leaves, twigs,
And listen to my friends the larks and hummingbirds,
Woodpeckers and cardinals,
Doves and starlings."

"Dost thou dress a certain way
That I could know for certain it is Thee?"

"I like to tie my hair in bunches
Or let it blow loose in the breeze.
I like skinny pants and warm fuzzy tops
In the cold times

"And soft cottony caftans,
Nightgown sheer and swishy,
When it's warm,
Or long goddess-like gowns
With ruana shawls."

## 16

"What would someone who does not know thee
Notice first?"

"My boyish child-like demeanor
Belying an impish sensual subtle woman inside."

 "Ah," Jai observes, "so thou movest between girl and woman,
Imp and goddess."

"Thou hast got it!"

Jai ventures, "And art thou vain."

"I don't relate to that word at all!
Maybe I just get a warm feeling
Of self-satisfaction
When a beloved really sees me
And loves me for no reason,
Beams in my presence.
Is that vain?
Not by my reckoning!"

"Dost thou have a special language or accent?"

"I adore speaking French, Spanish, and Thai.
But truly I am at the heart of all beings,
From all lands and cultures.
I am in the hearts of every being
Who shares this planet with me.
And when I speak those languages,
I turn into a Francaise, an Espagnola, a Thai."

"How so?"

"I become free, happy, liberated!
Quick to laugh!"

"How shall I call thee?
By what name?"

"O child, O woman, call me Thyself!"

And with that,
The being who told Jai to call her
"Thyself" disappears and is silent.

Now Jai is completely confused.

Again, Jai feels lost.
Where did her new mermaid/nymph-like friend go?
Where did Night/Knight go?
She wanders aimlessly,
Then decides to sit by a tree,
And ponder.

20

Her steed nuzzles her as if to say,
"This way! Follow me!"

Remaining mystified, but somehow reassured, she accepts his invitation
and once again upon her beloved horse, she sees at a distance
a scene she hasn't seen before,
steam rising from a body of water and angelic-like women.
She dismounts from the horse and walks closer.
Three women wearing white come to greet her.
They offer water to her horse first, then a glass of water to her.
She is grateful.

They invite her silently to an area where they will ready her for
The healing which she intuits she is to receive within the nearby Temple,
The Temple of Aesclepius, where all who enter receive a
Special dream, a gift, a guidance,
Which become a healing for those who enter willingly.

One of the women directs her to disrobe behind a screen so that they may pour water
Over her, before she will submerge herself in the pure waters of a healing pool.
This is a form of outer cleansing symbolic of her future inner cleansing.
When she steps out, another angelic-seeming woman dresses her

22

In sparkling white flowing garments
And leads her silently to the Temple.

## CHAPTER FOUR

# THE WAY IN: FEEDING THE SERPENTS

The woman explains to her that before one can enter the inner sanctum
Of the Temple and receive the healing dream or message,
One has to feed the serpents who dwell in the outskirts of the
Inner sanctum.
The serpents represent different aspects of her psyche which she will need to acknowledge before each one will transform.
The transformation will happen when she faces each serpent

And feeds each a honey-cake she will make herself.

The woman points to honey and flour indicating that she is
To make nine honeycakes to feed the nine snakes.
Jai balks and fear invades her being.
Can she trust this process or should she retreat?
She looks into the eyes of her horse. He nods.
She looks into the eyes of the woman guide who extends her hand.
Jai chooses to trust.
She takes a deep breath.
Her heart is beating fast and her body trembling.

She makes the honeycakes.
Before offering them, she is to look into the eyes of each snake.
In each, she will receive a reflection of her own shadow.
These are parts of her false self she needs to acknowledge,
Understand, befriend, and release.

She is led to the entry and then is on her own.
She finds some renewed inner strength,
Some strong desire to take this risk,
For the sake of her destiny, her self-revelation.

She slowly enters the precinct where she sees the first serpent.
She is scared.
But now she realizes that fear is the first shadow she needs to face
And transform: her fear of her own true self,
Of her innermost knowing, of her value.
She realizes she has had a tendency to devalue or ignore who she truly is
And what she is here to give to herself and the world.

It is time to feed this first serpent the first honey-cake.
She approaches him and talks to him as if he is her own inner child.
"I know you are fearful and that is perfectly natural.
But I am here to protect you and so to transform your fear when

"You are ready, into courage, confidence, and fearlessness.
I am here to recognize your value which is my true value
Reflecting back to me through you."

As soon as the snake swallows the honey-cake, instantly there is
A transformation.
He slithers around Jai, touching and gently caressing her skin.
It evokes an earth-centered warmth, sensuality, and relaxation
Into herself, including a self-acceptance and embrace of her
Womanhood. And she knows that this is good.

In fact, as soon as the snake slithers away, she feels as if a long-time burden
Has been lifted from her heart, from her history.

The second snake appears. The snake and Jai lock eyes. She looks away.
Then she looks back and moves closer to her.
This female snake appears to be angry, annoyed, resentful,
And Jai recognizes these extreme emotions as her own.
As soon as her recognition surfaces, she is able to hold out the
Honey-cake. The serpent takes it, eats it, and Jai feels a new lightness of heart,
Inner peace, and freedom from those excesses of negativity.
The lightness even morphs into forgiveness of herself and others
And understanding.

The serpent vanishes into a distant invisible corner.

When the third serpent appears, she faces aspects of need and greed.
He represents her own subconscious tendencies to hoard
And cling onto what she no longer needs but is scared to release,
In case she may want these outmoded irrelevant possessions.
Once she acknowledges that she wants to be free of these once and for all,
She feeds him the honey-cake and in so doing,
A sense of generosity and gratitude for what she has and what she is
Fills her and she senses once again into her enough-ness,
Free from distorted beliefs about lack and insecurity.

And she feels a new sense of lightness and even a desire to dance,
The snake even becomes a lithe dancer, light-hearted and buoyant,
And so does Jai. And then this serpent slithers away.

The fourth serpent confronts her with a display of jealousy,
And though Jai feels the sense of enough-ness from
The previous experience, she realizes there are still more old memories to release,
In the form of this negative emotion.
She knows the antidote; it is appreciation.
As soon as that realization arises in her, she can feed the serpent

And all is transformed.
She remembers all those past and present who have given her
Something beneficial, whether material or spiritual,
And feels how deeply appreciative, grateful, and fortunate she is,
And again, the serpent goes on his way.

The fifth snake barely looks at Jai. She looks away; this snake represents Jai's shyness,
her need to hide or be secretive, her discomfort with visibility.
She offers the honeycake and the fifth snake turns into a strong self-possessed nymph,
smiling, straightforward, no longer shy and hidden.
She merges herself into Jai and these qualities are now hers.
Even more excitement arises than before and
Ja feels hopeful for what she knows not.
If such a habitual feeling of needing to hide can transform like this,
Who knows what else can benefit her?

The sixth snake glares at her, and
reminds her of her judgmentalism,
her narrowness and closed-mindedness,
her self-righteousness. She befriends him with the honeycake and he instantly releases
Jai from these habitual negativities and becomes a partner with whom to dance and
engage with elegant mutual respect, an honoring of collaboration, and

listening so that no one point of view acts to control the other.
She begins to enjoy more fully than before a new lightness of being.

The seventh snake bears an excessively serious demeanor,
joyless, and even glum, unable to laugh or feel bliss, just like Jai sometimes.
Again, the honeycake works wonders, and this snake transforms into a diva with a glass of wine in one hand and a singing voice which brings all hearers including Jai into a deep and subtle internal bliss.
The song becomes her own and the voice hers to keep.
And she smiles with inner self-satisfaction and joy.

The eighth nearly last snake reveals her lazy streak,
some kind of inertia, or reluctance to go forth into its destiny, Jai's destiny.
Furthermore, the snake shows Jai that part of this inertia is because she does not know how to prioritize or use her time well.
The snake needs to eat this next to last honeycake and point out to Jai the path to her canvas, paints, paintbrush, as well as her harp and her pens and paper --
As the way of the Creatrice.
As soon as she eats the honeycake, there is energy, purpose,
a turning toward her North Star,
a new knowing for Jai that becomes a possibility for manifesting instantly.
At last she has a glimpse of the Way that has been forever meant for her

in order to enter the domain of her true being.
Jai bows before this snake in recognition and gratitude.

The ninth serpent appears as her egoic tendency to think that she is the "only one," apart from everyone else, the one who knows the truth, who can get "what I want when I want it!" More than that, she comes to realize her ego comes from her deep-seated belief in being a separate identity, someone special, not needing to acknowledge her interdependence with others and all of Nature as essential to her existence, her well-being.

With this recognition, as she understands that all are interconnected and united in oneness, she lets her illusory sense of separateness vanish. As a result, the serpent who receives her offering of the honey-cake recedes into another area of the sanctum, and instantly, all is transformed. She has the veils removed from the eyes of her belief systems. She feels a sense of inner spaciousness, clarity, clear-seeing, and an awareness which used to be hidden but is now more evident and present.

She senses into the Oneness of all that is, and though this is a temporary awakening, this will allow her to be extraordinarily receptive to the dream-healing she is about to receive once she enters the inner sanctum, the question she is still holding in her deepest self—"Am I complete as Day without my Night/Knight? Or do I need him to be complete?"

34

Jai is now ready to enter the inner sanctum, feeling empowered by having faced her nine shadows, and willing to receive whatever is meant for her. She has become calm, peaceful, and open to what is next.

## CHAPTER FIVE
# INCUBATING THE DREAM

The angelic woman is pleased with Jai's progress
and directs her now to the slab where she is to lie down and sleep,
but only in order to witness a lucid dream
which will provide the healing she is there to receive.
Harpists circle round her,
Playing their lyres, all night long.

The lyre-players lull her to sleep with their flowing unfamiliar sounds.
She will soon fall asleep,
And dream exquisite lucid dreams.

Just before she falls into a deep sleep, she says to herself,
"I am Day in search of my Night. I feel incomplete without my Night."

39

But within a short time, Jai enters into a deep state of rest.
Her limbs relaxed, her third eye allows her to dream travel.

She says to herself in her dream, "I wander through hill and vale and
ride through the sky on an invisible magic carpet.
I am landing in a vast forest where a grand baobab tree
With a large opening in its trunk is inviting me to enter."

She begins to feel enveloped in a velvety darkness which warms her
And comforts every inch on her body.

"My search for Night ends here," she murmurs in her sleep/dream.
"I need not know how or why, but I feel Day has at last met the one who completes me."

Night is replete with wonders and blessings.
Day is overflowing in gratitude.

She smiles in her sleep and opens her heart, arms, and whole being as Night makes love to all of her, head to toe, including her electro-magnetic field, her subtle bodies, and all of her energy centers.
No part is left out.

She rests there for a long time which is truly a timeless dimension.
She is after all in a Temple of eternal significance.

She is in awe, without words.
As she lies in the sacred depths of Night, inside the cavern of this huge tree,
The space she rests in expands and grows.

It is a friendly darkness, a loving response to her deepest longing,
To find her Night, her Knight, and discover the answer to her long-time
Unanswerable question:
"Am I Day whole unto myself?
Or do I need my Night, my Knight in order to complete who
And what I am?"

Here in this ever-expanding inner sanctum of the tree, she wakes up.
She realizes, "I am both, I am a Presence, an Awareness that is
Ever awake, an unburdened, accepting free spirit.
I become the eternal emptiness of open sky-heart as Day and at the same time,
I abide in and as Night,
the all-pervading intimacy of Night,
The all-inclusive embrace of my Knight.

"I am lying in this Divine embrace aware of its indelible imprint.
I, Day, whose earthly name is Jai, will never again be lonely,
Bereft, all alone.
Instead, I will ever feel the perennial company of the One,

"My Night-Knight lover.
I am one with the One.
My aloneness becomes a resounding 'Yes' to all Oneness."

She carries this Oneness-awareness as she hears the melodies of the lyres slowly bring her out of the lucid dream state.
It is the moment when Night becomes Dawn.
She has been dreaming the whole night long and now
She is filled with the gift of her dream
Which has healed her of all dichotomies, false beliefs, illusions.

She who calls herself Day is now able to sit up
And beam love from her night-blessed daylight sparkling eyes
And heart. She smiles at the lovely dedicated lyre-players,
Swings her legs over the marble slab and stands up.
She feels as if she has grown as tall as the heavens.
She also feels extended down as deep as the core of Mother Earth.
This verticality of energy allows her to feel like a bridge
Between heaven and earth.
She feels energized and powerful and ready to return to her home.

She turns to thank the lyre players.
They acknowledge her silently.

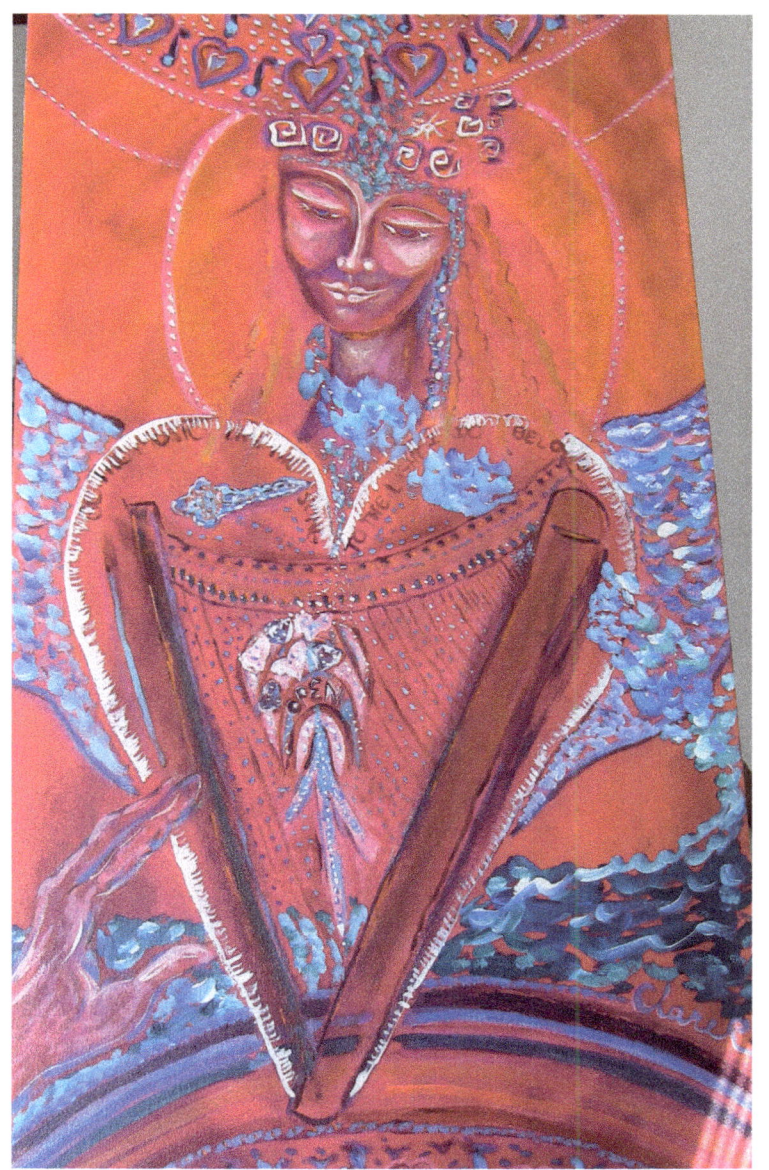

She walks a few steps to the outer sanctum and looks for the serpents
To offer her thanks to them, too.
They seem to have vanished.

She walks out the door from the Aesclepius Temple
And silently bows in reverence to Aesclepius,
That wondrous healer of the Greek mysteries and medical arts of ancient times,
Son of Apollo, whose snake-entwined staff, the caduceus,
Is the symbol of medicine for all time.

She walks in a harmonious flow to greet the women
Who bathed and clothed her.
They give each other a silent knowing acknowledgement.
They recognize the profound changes occurring in her.
She changes into her own clothes which the women kept for her.

She now looks up to find her trusty steed, her beloved, awaiting her.
She is grateful.

## CHAPTER SIX

# HOMECOMING

She climbs upon his welcoming back and they gallop off
Toward the land of her first birth,
Aware that she is now experiencing a second birth,
A rebirth and a newfound commitment to listen deeply
To the promptings of her heart, the messages of her dreams, and the synchronicities
That Will invite her to act wisely and bravely in this earthly realm
To which she is returning.

While riding the horse, she exclaims aloud with great joy,
"I am Day and I am Night!
I am Fullness and I am Emptiness!
I am Earth and I am Heaven!
I am Alone and I am all One!
I am Form and I am Formless!

"I am Nowhere and I am Everywhere!
I am No One and I am Everyone!"

In gratitude, Jai feels she will live the miracle of this newfound Awakening
For the rest of her days and the rest of her nights.

## CHAPTER SEVEN

# MEETING HER MUSE

Now once she returns home,
she senses a sweet feminine presence calling out to her.
She cannot hear her yet.
Jai asks, "Are you the girl I met before I found my way?"

"Yes, I am the one who told you that
I am in your heart, in your pen,
In your paintbrush, inside your canvas, in your own songs, and
In your deepest longings," she answers.

"How would I recognize you now?"

"Only when you flesh me out in words or paint
Or musical notes. You could catch me in a flash memory
Of a dream or an alchemical journey.

"In case you do not realize it yet,
I am your Muse, your Legendary Self,
Your Divine Creatrice."

"I am so happy to recognize you at last as my very own Self.
You see, I'm letting you as me
And me as you
Out of hiding in these words."

"Yes, Jai, I'm ecstatic for that."

"Do we now have special powers? A knack for something?"

"Oh yes, I heal when called upon,
I find lost items,
I resurrect stanzas of prayers
Long forgotten.
I also resurrect lost souls,
Lost to themselves,
Hopeless and at wit's end.
I awaken them to their genius."

"Just as you are awakening me
To mine?"

"Yes, dear one."

"Are there some special characters you turn into
Which are aspects of my Legendary Self?"

"Oh yes, the hermit --you like your solitude and your
Silent prayer time, right?"

"Yes, for sure. I like to stay apart and ponder, write, paint, or
Play my harp in cloistered sacred space."

"And the alchemist…"

"Yes, one of my highest intents is
The transformation of consciousness
Through light, love, peace, equanimity,
The healing arts, music, and being
A blessingful presence in the world."

"Yes, that is why we are together.
And there is one more aspect or character,
As you say."

"What is that?"

"The dancer, the lover, the one
In love with life."

"Oh yes, that's the one in me who is
Ever so latent and clamoring to reveal herself,"
Jai exclaims.

"Yes, I am here to help you make sure
She emerges.
I am that lithe slithery sensuality
In motion.
I am on the inmost lining
Of your very own limbs.
Feel me!
Lean into me!
Allow yourself to surrender to Thyself!"

The night is studded with stars
And it is only halfway over.
Jai remains dialogue with her Legendary Self.

"Do you get up in the morning and go to bed at night?"

"Oh, little one," she answers, recognizing a new divinity
Arising in her dreaming partner.

She begins to speak in her ancient 'thee" and "thou" language-
"I am eternally awake!
If thou wouldst cognize my presence, thou wouldst know
Thy oneness with me, thy Legendary Self,
And this knowledge would urge thee to awaken
And rise up with energy and happiness each morn.
And when thou returnest to bed at night,
Thou wouldst feel my being stretched out in Thee."

"Oh, now we are becoming united!" Jai cries out.

"Yes, and I know that sometimes thou used to go to thy bed
To weep and shake with sorrows.
But I want thee to know that I am ever holding thee
Throughout,
Never ever have I abandoned thee;
Only thou hast not known of my presence."

"Now that I know, I will remember."

There is a time of silence as Jai absorbs
All that she is receiving.
Then she asks, "Are you real or a fairytale character?"

"How could I not be real?
Dost remember Ka-Ela the goddess in thy story
Of the Call of Mother Earth?
It is I the being of Light who hears her call
And floats down to earth to invite the villagers
And teach them how to heal her."

"Oh, and are you Nameless One of Splendor,
The Creatrice I wrote about who is the
Divine Feminine Creative Force of the world?"

"Oh, yes, I am all that thou hast thought
And spoken and written that is filled
With high ideals and poetic beauty."

"I am glad to hear this.
What do you really believe in,

"My Legendary Self?"

"In creativity, ingenuity, newness of thinking,
Evolution of consciousness,
Transformation of humanity from smallness of outlook
To largesse of infinite perspectives,
From narrow racist attitudes

"To vast heart-centered inclusivity
Of diverse individuals of all paths
And ethnic groups.
I believe in the subsiding and ending
Of greed and power-mongering
And the arising of generosity and cooperativeness.

"I, indwelling the depths of Thee, believe in
Letting go and sharing, in moving humanity from
Judging and condemning
To discerning and accepting,
From grief to joy."

"Those are precisely my deepest longings and concerns!
You have truly expressed my True Self."

"Yes, my beloved, that is why thou hast journeyed to the healing Temple of Aesclepius.
Now that Thou art back in your home,
Thou art ready to claim forever the healing thou hast been given, essentially
The truth of thine own being accepted and honored and allowed to
Come alive and be fully manifested. "

"Oh thank you, cherished one, my twin self, the Being of my Being!
How can I ever fully appreciate and acknowledge you?"

"Recognize my dear, that thou art thine own Knight of Thy night!
The One thou hast been seeking all these lifetimes!
The wholeness thou gavest away to thy imaginary Knight!"

"Oh, but there will be times when I do long for my Knight,
The one who will love me as an earthly woman,
The one who will act as my other half, and yet now I will recognize
That he too is complete in himself, and together,
We will be two wholenesses – a chance to shine upon the world
And beam out like a sun our essential radiance."

"Yes, and now thou dost understand what the Sun was trying to tell thee
Before thou didst set out on your journey to find the Knight of thy night!"

"Yes, and I not only have a great renewed love for the Sun and Light and Joy,
But I learned from the snakes how to see my own dark corners and unhealthy habits
And to transform them, not by looking away, but by facing their darkness fully
And being paradoxically enlightened by the process!"

"Yes, my dear, and now it is time to awaken to the fact that thou art no longer a needy
Seeker, But now a renewed enlivened human Prophetess and Creatrice and Finder
Of the hidden and revealed, no longer in the dark, yet valuing it greatly,
No longer unfulfilled, but fully filled and embodied as an instrument of the Divine,
As a bringer of Goodness, Truth, and Beauty to all beings,
As a creator of Love, Harmony, and Divinity wherever thou goest!"

"Thank you! O thank you! Will you be my inner guide and companion for the rest of my days?"

"Here I am, ever-present! Look within and there thou wilt find all thou wouldst seek!"

"I will! I am Thy very own Innermost! I am here for Thee from lifetime to lifetime! Enter Thy depths which is the true Jai, the true Heart, the true Thy very own Self, and I will be ever-present! Jai, thou art the Day of thy Night, and the Knight of thy Day!! Thou hast uncovered the secret Thou sought!"

"Godspeed, dear one! Godspeed!"

# About The Author

Clare Rosenfield is a former French teacher, licensed clinical social worker, artist, poet, writer, and harpist as well as the President of a non-profit called Global Healing Foundation.

Recently, she has published the following children's books: *Seven Meditations for Children, SUN-CHILD, The Story of Liliana: A Brave Indigenous Child, The Sleeping*

*Giantess Wakes Up, The Little Girl Who Wanted to be a Tree,* and *To The Rescue: Little Creatures: How Do I Love Thee?*

Her seven self-illustrated poetry collections include: *Dance upon the winds swept cloudless, Roll On Great Earth, The Call of Mother Earth: How a Being of Light Draws Forth Humanity's Response, Nameless One of Splendor: Her Sacred Arts of Creation, Tall Grasses of Woods Hole & Other Summery Poems, Ninsun: Wise Mother of Gilgamesh,* and *Your Inmost Tree of Life: An Invitation*.

Her personal website is www.contacthealing.com
Her non-profit Global Healing Foundation website is www.globalhealingfoundation.org

www.ingramcontent.com/pod-product-compliance
Lightning Source LLC
LaVergne TN
LVHW072019060526
838200LV00062B/4899